Allah Gave Me

TWO HANDS
AND FEET

ISBN 0 86037 348 7

MUSLIM CHILDREN'S LIBRARY

ALLAH THE MAKER SERIES

Allah Gave Me Two Hands And Feet

Author: *Raana Bokhari*
Illustrator: *Asiya Clarke*
Designer: *Steven Stratford*

Published by
The Islamic Foundation
Markfield Conference Centre
Ratby Lane, Markfield
Leicester LE67 9SY
United Kingdom
T (01530) 244 944
F (01530) 244946
E i.foundation@islamic-foundation.org.uk

Quran House, PO Box 30611, Nairobi, Kenya

PMB 3193, Kano, Nigeria

British Library Cataloguing in Publication Data

Printed by Imak Ofset, Turkey

British Library Cataloguing in Publication Data

Bokhari, Raana
Allah Gave me two hands and feet. - (Allah the maker series)
1. Touch - Juvenile literature 2. Touch - Religious aspects -
Islam - Juvenile literature 3. Hand - Juvenile literature
4. Foot - Juvenile literature 5. Hand - Religious aspects -
Islam - Juvenile literature 6. Foot - Religious aspects -
Islam - Juvenile literature
I. Title II. Islamic Foundation
612.8'8
ISBN 0860373487

Allah Gave Me

TWO HANDS AND FEET

Raana Bokhari

Illustrated by Asiya Clarke

THE ISLAMIC FOUNDATION

Allah gave me two hands to feel
So many wonderful things.

My Mummy's soft face, her dress and its lace,
And the joy that cuddling her brings.

Allah gave me two hands to touch with
As my brother and I play with toys!

But he tickles my tummy, so I run to Mummy,
'Enough of being silly now, boys!'

Allah gave me two hands to squeeze,
Soft, furry, and prickly leaves.

They're red and green, such a sight to be seen!
Watch me pick them from those tall trees!

Allah gave me two hands to eat with,
Lovely food, delicious and filling.

Soft strawberries, hard apples, pastry, warm falafels!
Ooh! To eat them all I'm only too willing!

9

Allah gave me two hands to pray with,
As I stand and bow in prayer.

I raise them to thank Him, praise and love Him,
Promising to always be kind and fair.

Allah gave me two feet to walk with
Through the soft warm sand by the sea.

The water tickles my toes, and trickles,
As we all splash about, Mum, Dad and me.

13

Allah gave me two feet to run with
To the ice cream van in my street.

I feel so jolly, as I eat my ice lolly,
Jumping and skipping on my podgy feet.

Allah gave me two feet to kick with,
As I play in the fields with my ball.

I dribble and flick it, tackle and kick it,
And hey everyone! It's a goal!

Allah gave me two feet to feel
The soft earth and grass so cool.

18

What a beautiful sight, glowing in the light,
With flowers like pretty bright jewels.

Allah gave me two feet to walk with
To the mosque as I hurry to pray.

I stand on my feet, in the cold and the heat,
And thank Allah for my life, every day!

Other books in the Series

Allah Gave Me
Two Eyes to See

The Food We Eat

Animals

Allah Gave Me
Two Hands And Feet

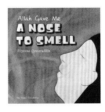

Allah Gave Me
A Nose to Smell

Allah Gave Me
A Tongue to Taste

Allah Gave Me
Two Ears to Hear

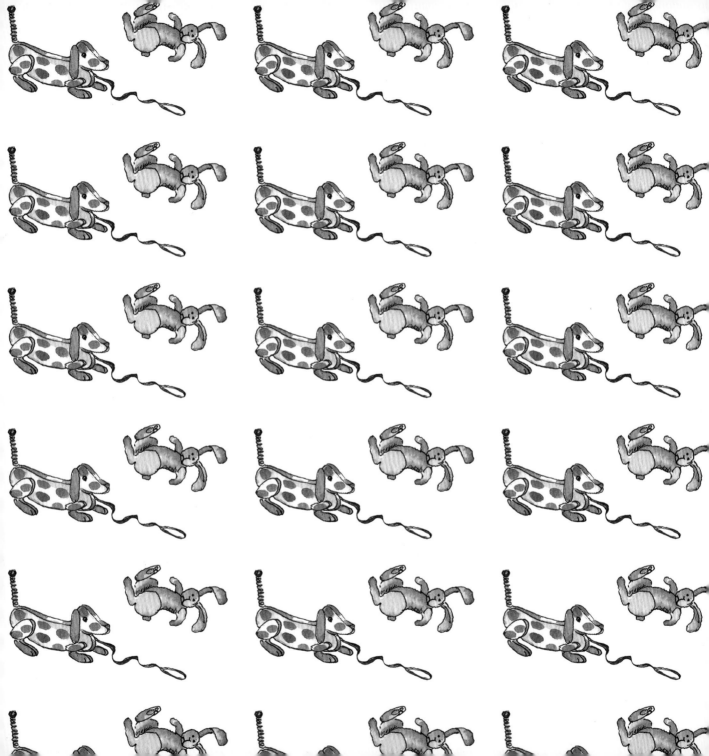